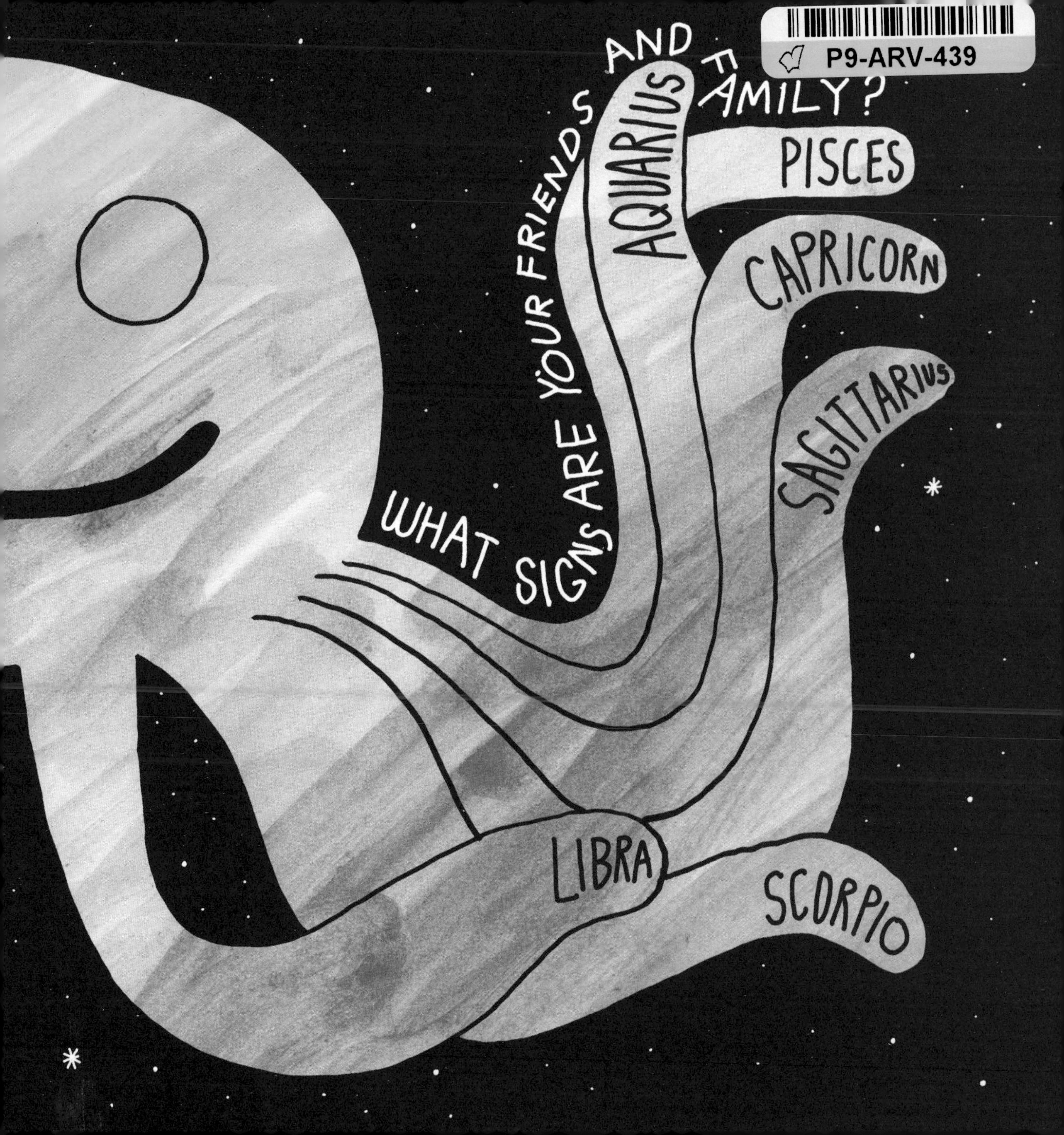
WHAT SIGNS ARE YOUR FRIENDS AND FAMILY?
AQUARIUS
PISCES
CAPRICORN
SAGITTARIUS
LIBRA
SCORPIO

ILLUSTRATED BY MIKE PERRY

ASTRO BABY

BY MICHELLE TEA

dottir press
NEW YORK CITY

FOR ATTICUS, OF COURSE!

Published in 2019 by Dottir Press
33 Fifth Avenue
New York, NY 10003

Dottirpress.com

First printing April 2019

Production by Drew Stevens

Trade distribution by Consortium Book Sales and Distribution, www.cbsd.com. For inquiries about bulk sales, please contact jb@dottirpress.com.

Library of Congress Cataloging-in-Publication Data is available for this title.
ISBN 978-1-948340-07-6

Printed in Malaysia by Tien Wah Press, December 2018

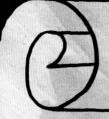

THE MOMENT YOU WERE BORN,
TIME STOOD STILL
AND YOUR CHART WAS CAST
WITH A MAGICAL QUILL.

THE STARS AND THE PLANET
BEGAN TO PLAY—
AND LEFT THEIR MARK ON
YOUR SPECIAL DAY.

NOW SOME OF THE WAYS YOU LAUGH AND FROWN REFLECT THE ENERGY THEY BEAMED DOWN,

AND AS YOU CONTINUE TO LEARN AND GROW, ASTROLOGY CAN HELP YOU KNOW

ARIES!

RULED BY THE

AND THE ELEMENT OF *FIRE*

PLANET

MARS

ASTRO BABY ARIES IS A RAM!

TAURUS!

*

RULED BY THE

PLANET

VENUS

AND THE ELEMENT OF EARTH

ASTRO BABY TAURUS IS A BULL!

GEMINI !

RULED BY THE

AND THE ELEMENT OF AIR

PLANET

MERCURY

ASTRO BABY GEMINI IS THE TWINS!

THE GEMINI TWINS LIKE TO BABBLE AND CHAT.
THEY'RE USUALLY LIKE THIS, BUT THEY'RE OFTEN LIKE THAT:

CANCER!

RULED BY THE

AND THE ELEMENT OF WATER .

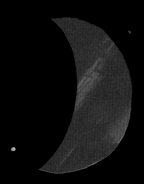

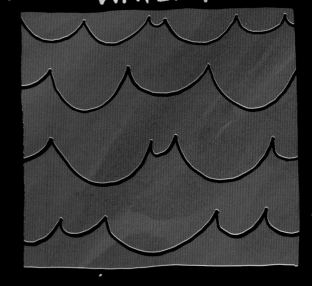

MOON

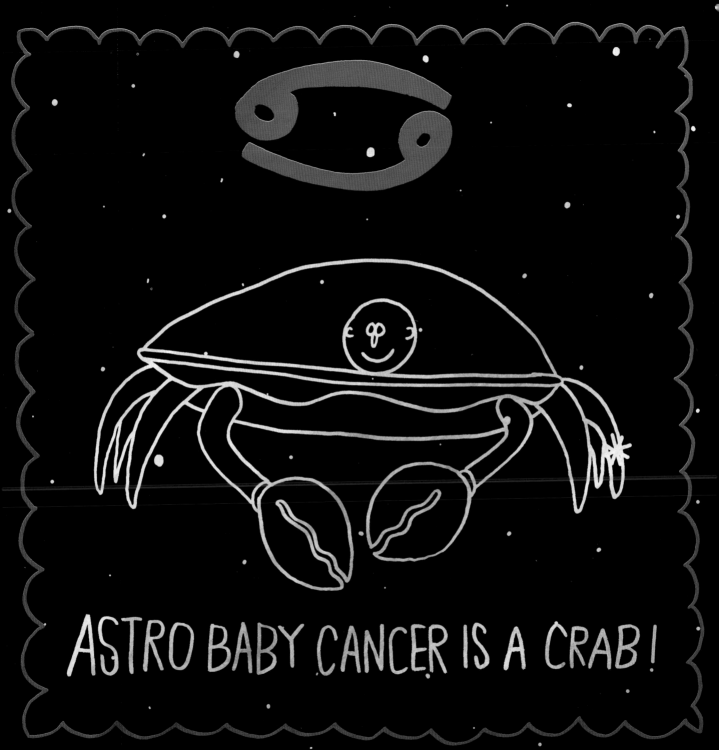

ASTRO BABY CANCER IS A CRAB!

WITH BIG CRABBY CLAWS,
CANCER BABY HOLDS TIGHT,

AND FOLLOWS HIS HEART
WITH ALL OF HIS MIGHT.

THIS SENSITIVE BABY
CAN BE SHY AND QUIET,
THEN TURN GIGGLE-SILLY,
A TUMBLING LAUGH RIOT!

LEO!

RULED BY THE

AND THE ELEMENT OF
FIRE

SUN

ASTRO BABY LEO IS A* LION!

VIRGO!

RULED BY THE

PLANET

MERCURY

AND THE ELEMENT OF
EARTH

ASTRO BABY VIRGO IS VIRTUOUS!

LIBRA!

ULED BY THE

AND THE ELEMENT OF
AIR

PLANET

VENUS

ASTRO BABY LIBRA IS . THE SCALES

SCORPIO!

*

RULED BY THE

AND THE ELEMENT OF WATER

PLANET

PLUTO

ASTRO BABY SCORPIO IS A SCORPION!

*SAGITTARIUS!

RULED BY THE

PLANET

JUPITER

AND THE ELEMENT OF FIRE

ASTRO BABY SAGITTARIUS IS A CENTAUR!

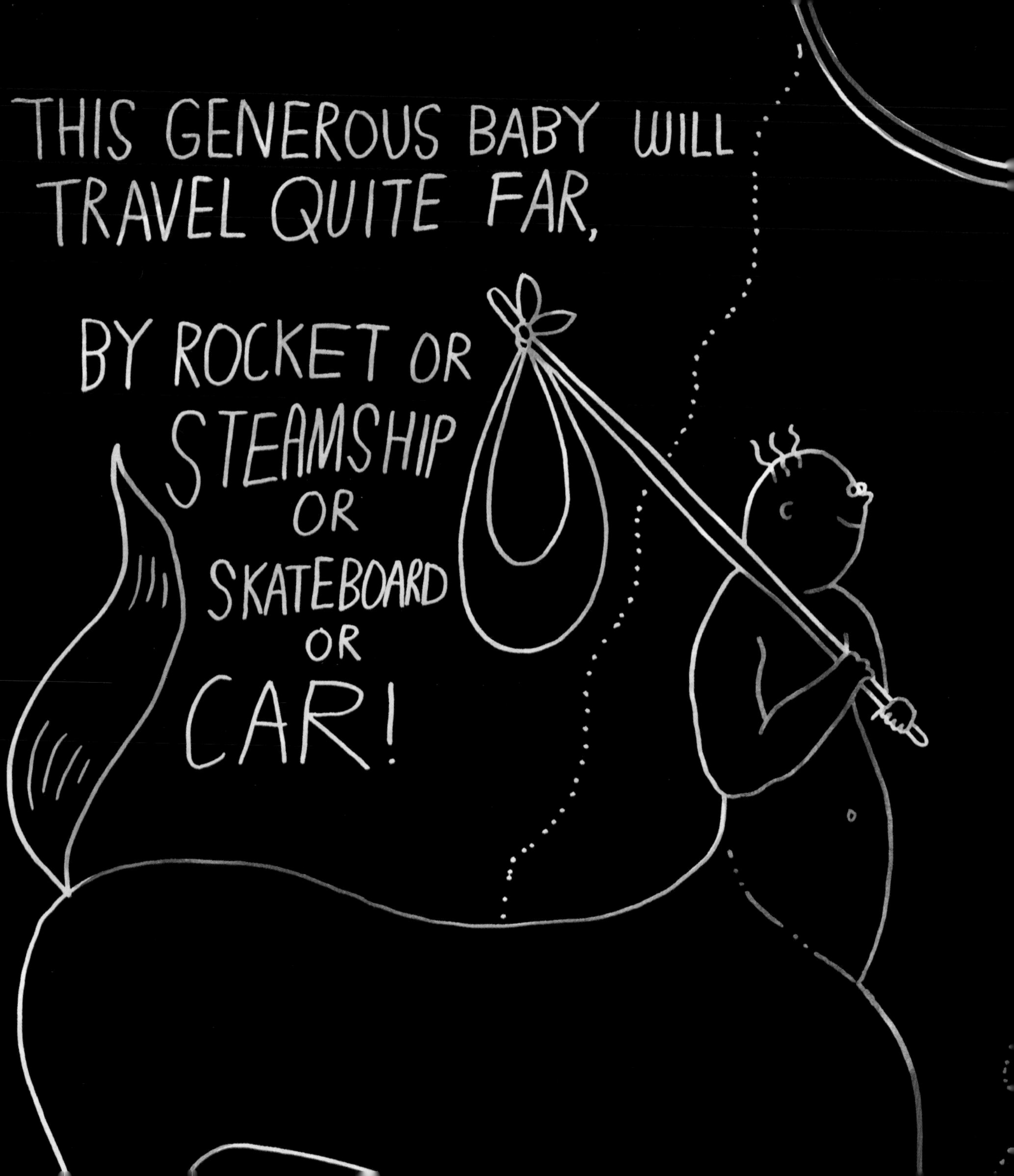
THIS GENEROUS BABY WILL
TRAVEL QUITE FAR,
BY ROCKET OR
STEAMSHIP
OR
SKATEBOARD
OR
CAR!

CAPRICORN!

RULED BY THE

AND THE ELEMENT OF
EARTH

PLANET

{ • SATURN • }

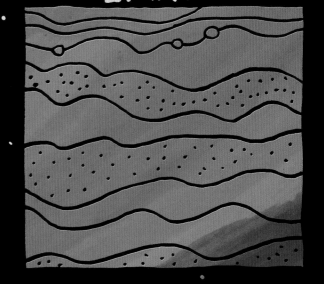

ASTRO BABY CAPRICORN
IS A MOUNTAIN GOAT !

WHILE OTHER BABIES STUMBLE AND CRAWL ABOUT DROOLING,
THIS SERIOUS GOAT HAS MASTERED WORLD-RULING!

AQUARIUS!

RULED BY THE

AND THE **ELEMENT OF** AIR

PLANET

URANUS

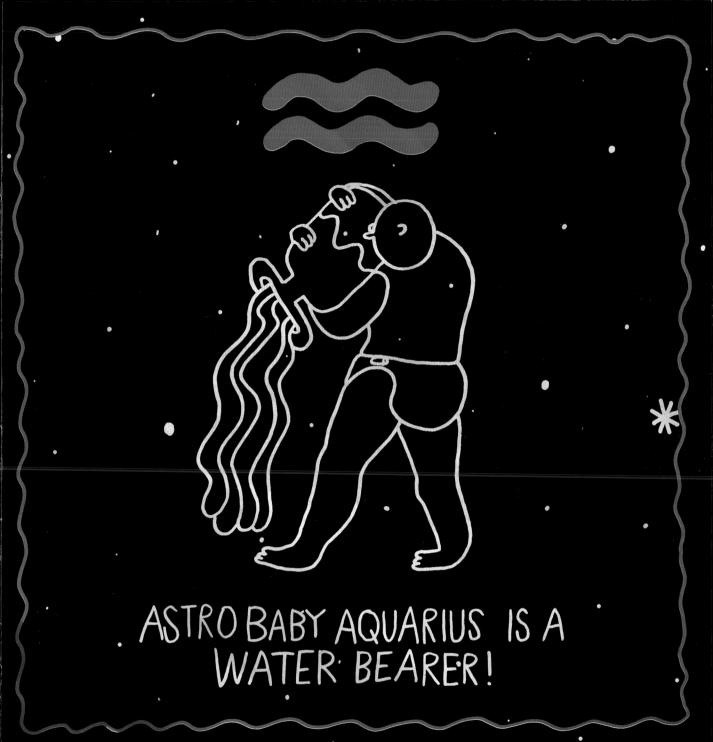

ORIGINAL AQUARIUS IS CHOCK-FULL OF STORIES, FROM FAIRY TALE DREAMSCAPES TO OUTERSPACE GLORIES.

FROM UP IN THE STARS
SHE SHARES VISION AND HOPE,

THIS WATER BEARER
BABY DOESN'T HEAR THE
WORD "NOPE!"

PISCES!

RULED BY THE

PLANET

AND THE ELEMENT OF WATER

NEPTUNE

ASTRO BABY PISCES IS A FISH!

LOVELY BABY PISCES IS WISE
WITH COMPASSION,
AND LIKES TO EXPRESS HIMSELF
WITH ART, CRAFTS, AND FASHION.

A MOST FRIENDLY FISH,
HE WELCOMES ALL TO HIS SCHOOL,
AND KNOWS THAT OUR FEELINGS
ARE WHAT MAKE US COOL!

THE END...

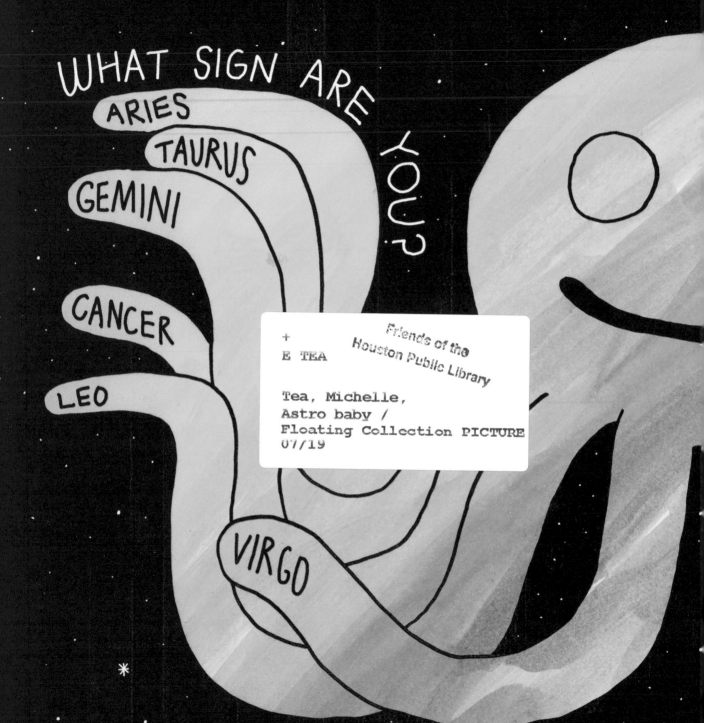